Jessica's Bad Dream

"There's a giant fish in the lake!" Jessica
yelled. She picked up the oars of the rowboat
and tried to row. The boat wouldn't move.
The monster fish was catching up to her.

Suddenly, Jessica woke up and sat up in
bed. The room was very dark. Her heart was
pounding.

"What's wrong?" Elizabeth asked.

Jessica took a deep breath. She was still
scared. "Nothing," she whispered. It sounded
silly to say she was being chased by a fish.
Besides, she didn't want her sister to know
she was afraid. "I was having a bad dream."

Jessica curled up under the covers again
and closed her eyes. She definitely wasn't
going fishing now.

SWEET VALLEY KIDS

JESSICA AND THE JUMBO FISH

Written by
Molly Mia Stewart

Created by
FRANCINE PASCAL

Illustrated by
Ying-Hwa Hu

A BANTAM SKYLARK BOOK®
NEW YORK · TORONTO · LONDON · SYNDEY · AUCKLAND

RL 2, 005–008

JESSICA AND THE JUMBO FISH
A Bantam Skylark Book / June 1991

Sweet Valley High™ and Sweet Valley Kids are registered trademarks of Francine Pascal

Conceived by Francine Pascal

Produced by Daniel Weiss Associates, Inc.
33 West 17th Street
New York, NY 10011

Cover art by Susan Tang

ISBN 0-553-15936-4

Published simultaneously in the United States and Canada

Bantam Books are published by Bantam Books, a division of Bantam Doubleday Dell Publishing Group, Inc. Its trademark, consisting of the words "Bantam Books" and the portrayal of a rooster, is Registered in U.S. Patent and Trademark Office and in other countries. Marca Registrada. Bantam Books, 666 Fifth Avenue, New York, New York 10103.

To Jane Elizabeth Chardiet

CHAPTER 1

Seasick

Jessica Wakefield sat down on her bed and hugged her stuffed koala bear. "I don't want to go," she said.

"Don't be so grouchy," her twin sister, Elizabeth, said. "You've been telling me that all week. If you go, you'll see that fishing is really fun."

Jessica and Elizabeth were packing their suitcases. The whole family was going on a weekend fishing trip to celebrate Mr. Wakefield's birthday. Mr. Wakefield was always telling the twins and their brother, Steven, about the fishing trips he took when he was a boy. Elizabeth and Steven thought they sounded great. Jessica didn't.

"Fishing isn't fun!" Jessica said. "You have to touch worms. Besides, if we go out on a boat, I'll get seasick."

"What's wrong with worms?" Elizabeth sat down next to Jessica and wriggled her fingers against Jessica's neck. "Worms like you."

"Stop it!" Jessica said, trying to get away. She was laughing, but she shivered, too.

Elizabeth liked worms. Jessica hated worms. That was just one of the differences between them. Elizabeth and Jessica were identical twins. They looked exactly the same on the outside, but they were very different inside. Elizabeth liked playing games outdoors, reading, and doing homework.

Jessica preferred playing with her dollhouse and watching cartoons on TV. She hated getting her clothes dirty. The only thing she liked about school was seeing her friends.

Jessica and Elizabeth both had blue-green eyes and long blond hair with bangs. They wore their name bracelets as often as possible, so people could tell them apart.

Being twins was special. Jessica and Elizabeth shared a bedroom and they shared secrets. Even though they liked different things, they were best friends.

"Besides, we aren't using worms for bait," Elizabeth said as she folded her nightgown. "Dad said we would use little pieces of meat."

"I *still* don't want to go," Jessica said. She hugged her koala bear tighter. It wasn't just the worms and the boat that bothered her. She hated the idea of touching the scaly

3

bodies of the fish and seeing their bulging eyes. She hated the idea of fishing so much that she decided at that moment to try to stay home. "I have to tell Mom something," she said as she hopped off her bed.

Jessica walked out of their bedroom to their parents' room. Mr. and Mrs. Wakefield were packing, too.

"Mom?" Jessica began. She tried to make her voice sound as weak as possible.

"What is it, honey? Do you need any help packing?" her mother asked.

Jessica put her arms around her stomach. "Mom, I don't feel well. I think I'm getting a stomachache."

"Hmm." Mr. Wakefield walked over and felt Jessica's forehead. "Are you getting sick?"

Jessica nodded. "I guess that means we

4

can't go, right? I'll have to stay in bed until I get better."

Elizabeth walked into the room. She looked surprised. "You didn't tell me you felt sick."

"It just started," Jessica said. She knew that wasn't exactly true. But she was so nervous about the trip that she was ready to try anything to get out of going—even telling a small lie.

"Do we have to miss the trip?" Elizabeth asked unhappily. She sounded very disappointed.

"What?" Steven, the twins' older brother, was standing in the doorway. He was in fourth grade. "We're not going?"

"I feel sick," Jessica explained.

Mrs. Wakefield snapped her suitcase shut. "I don't think you're too sick to travel, Jessica," she said. "You'll feel better once we get into the car."

Jessica bit her lip and tried to *look* sick. She opened her eyes very wide. "No, I won't," she said.

"Faker," Steven said. He punched her in the arm.

"Ouch." Jessica stuck out her tongue at her brother.

"I was afraid we wouldn't get to go," Elizabeth said with a sigh of relief.

Mr. Wakefield put his arm around Jessica's shoulders. "We'll roll the window down in the car. You'll feel great with the wind in your face. Now let's start packing up the car."

Everyone began to carry their bags downstairs, while Jessica lagged behind. She had not been able to get her parents to cancel the trip, but that didn't mean she was going to do any fishing. She would go on the trip with them, but she wouldn't get near a fishing pole—ever!

CHAPTER 2

Grouchy Jessica

Elizabeth climbed into the car and buckled her seat belt. "I can't wait to get to the lake!" she said excitedly. "This is going to be so much fun."

"You're going to love it up at Sun Lake," Mr. Wakefield said as he backed the car down the driveway. "All the cabins are right by the water, and each one has its own dock. We'll have a rowboat, too."

Steven rolled down his window. "I'm going to catch the biggest fish in the lake," he bragged.

"Good, then we won't go hungry," Mrs. Wakefield said, laughing.

"We won't anyway," Elizabeth reminded them. "Not with all the food we're bringing."

"And cooking outside will be neat," Steven said.

Jessica frowned. "Everything will get so dirty," she complained.

Elizabeth smiled at her sister. "No, it won't." She was sure Jessica would be in a better mood once they got to Sun Lake.

"You'll see beautiful birds up there," Mr. Wakefield said. "Ducks and swans—"

"Swans?" Jessica interrupted, leaning forward suddenly. "I love swans. I loved reading *The Ugly Duckling*."

"And little chipmunks come right up to

10

the picnic tables," Mrs. Wakefield added.

"Oh!" Jessica jumped up and down in her seat. "I want to see a chipmunk."

"How's that stomachache of yours?" Mr. Wakefield asked, looking at Jessica in the rearview mirror.

Jessica looked surprised for a moment. Then she hugged her stomach. "Oh, it hurts again," she said.

"You can stay in the cabin," Steven teased.

"Don't worry," Elizabeth said. "Lots of other families will be there. Maybe there will be some other kids in second grade."

"Maybe," Jessica said. "I hope some other kids hate fishing, too."

For the next two hours, they played Ghost and car Bingo, and they counted license plates from different states. The road twisted and turned up into the mountains. There were tall pine trees everywhere.

"Look! A deer!" Elizabeth said, pointing to a small clearing in the woods.

Jessica leaned forward, opening the window a bit more. "Oh! It's beautiful."

They continued to drive along the side of the mountain until a large blue lake came into sight.

"Wow!" Steven yelled. "Is that Sun Lake?"

"That's it," Mr. Wakefield said cheerfully. "It's just the way it's been since I was your age, Steven."

Elizabeth couldn't sit still. They turned onto a dirt road that went downhill among the trees. The air was cool and smelled of pine.

"When do you think we'll see the swans?"

Jessica wanted to know. "Can we feed them some bread?"

"Sure, honey," Mrs. Wakefield said. "The swans will probably be on the lake. Now everyone look for cabin number six."

"I've stayed there since I was a boy," Mr. Wakefield added.

Elizabeth, Jessica, and Steven looked out the windows at the cabins along the road. Each house was made of logs. Each had a chimney and a front porch with chairs.

"There it is!" Elizabeth shouted. "Cabin six!"

Mr. Wakefield pulled up in front of the cabin. Steven jumped out and ran to the door. Mr. Wakefield got out and stretched. Mrs. Wakefield smelled the clean air. "Isn't everything pretty?" she asked.

Elizabeth followed Jessica up the front path. Jessica was looking at the cabin next door. There were two boys sitting on the porch steps.

"Look!" Elizabeth said. "Those boys look like twins."

At that moment, the boys' cabin door opened, and a girl walked out onto the porch. She was carrying a doll.

"Hi," the girl said to Jessica and Elizabeth. She was wearing a pink sundress, clean white socks, and sneakers.

Jessica and Elizabeth leaned on their porch rail. "Hi, I'm Elizabeth, and this is my twin sister, Jessica," Elizabeth said.

"You're twins. My brothers are twins," the girl said. "My name is Jilly Crawford. Are you going fishing?"

Jessica quickly shook her head. "I'm not."

14

"Me neither," Jilly replied. "I hate to fish. It's too yucky."

Jessica gave Jilly a happy smile. All of a sudden she didn't feel grumpy anymore. It looked like she had found the perfect friend to play with at Sun Lake.

CHAPTER 3

Hook, Line, and Sinker

Jilly's brothers were talking to Steven. Their names were Tom and Ricky. "They've already caught lots of fish," Steven said to Elizabeth.

"And we're going to get a lot more," Tom said.

"So are we," Elizabeth said as she picked out her pole from the fishing gear her father had unloaded.

Mr. Wakefield walked out onto the porch. "Who feels like tossing in a line?"

"Me!" Elizabeth and Steven shouted at the same time.

Elizabeth put her hands in her pockets. "I'm going fishing," she said. "Are you sure you don't want to come, Jess?"

"My stomach still hurts," Jessica said. "I'd better not."

Elizabeth knew her sister was just using that excuse so she could stay behind and play with Jilly.

"OK," Elizabeth said.

"Let's go," Mr. Wakefield said. "Let's see how the fishing is from the dock."

"It's good," Ricky told them. "Can we come with you?"

Mr. Wakefield gave them a friendly smile. "Sure. Tell your parents, and then come join us. The more the merrier."

Elizabeth was so excited that she didn't mind Jessica's not coming. She couldn't wait to get her line in the water. "Come on, Dad," she said, running down to the dock.

When Elizabeth reached the edge of the water, she could see bugs walking back and forth along the water. Mr. Wakefield told her they were called water striders. Bits of lake weed floated on the surface of the water.

"I bet I'll get a bite on my first try," Steven said. He baited his hook and then showed Elizabeth how to bait hers.

"Maybe you will, maybe you won't," Elizabeth said with a laugh. "Remember Dad's birthday cake? You were bragging that yours would be better than mine and Jessica's, and it wasn't." The twins and Steven had made a

18

bet to see who would bake a better cake, and Steven had lost.

"I remember," Steven said. He sounded sad, but then he smiled. "Your cake did taste better, I guess."

"Now," said their father, "remember what we talked about, kids. Nice and steady casts, right?"

"Right," Elizabeth said.

Casting was the word for swinging the fishing pole so that the hook flew out across the water. Elizabeth put her pole to one side and then flicked it forward. The weight on the line, called the sinker, splashed into the water.

"Now reel it in gently and very slowly," Mr. Wakefield said.

Elizabeth started cranking the handle of

the wheel. The fishing line wound back up like a big spool of thread. "I didn't even get a nibble," she said. "My bait's still there." She got ready to try again. "This is fun!"

"Watch the expert," Steven said. He smiled to show he wasn't really bragging. Then he flicked his pole forward. The sinker landed neatly in the water.

Elizabeth practiced a few more times. It was fun sitting on the dock with her father and brother. The sun was starting to go down, and a cool breeze made the water ripple. Soon Tom and Ricky arrived and started casting their lines. Everything was quiet and peaceful.

Only one thing bothered Elizabeth. If they fished all weekend, they would catch a lot of fish. They couldn't eat fish for breakfast, lunch, and dinner.

"Dad?" she said. "Do we have to eat all the fish we catch?"

Mr. Wakefield was making a careful knot in his line to keep the hook on. "No," he said with a laugh. "We don't."

"Maybe we should throw back all the fish we know we won't be able to eat," Elizabeth suggested. "Then they can go back in the water and keep swimming."

"That's a good idea," Steven said.

"A very good idea," their father agreed.

Elizabeth smiled happily. She cast her line again and watched the hook fall into the water. Then she began reeling it in very slowly. Suddenly, she felt a tug.

"I think I have something!" she whispered.

Everyone stopped to watch her. She reeled in the line a little bit.

"It must be a big one!" Ricky said. "It looks heavy!"

Elizabeth gulped and turned the crank some more. Inch by inch, her line reeled in.

"It's going to be a real monster," Steven guessed.

"Nice and easy, Elizabeth. Nice and easy," Mr. Wakefield said.

With a tug, Elizabeth pulled her hook up out of the water. On the end was a large clump of weeds dripping with water.

"A real monster," Steven said with a laugh.

"More like a monster weed," Elizabeth said. She untangled the plants and dropped them back in the water.

They all cast their lines again. This time, Steven felt a tug. "I think I got one," he said with excitement.

They watched while he slowly reeled in his

line. Elizabeth crossed her fingers to wish him luck. She hoped they didn't all catch weeds.

Steven continued to reel in his line. Finally, a small fish came out of the water. "Yahoo!" he yelled. "I got one!"

"That's called a speckled trout and it looks to be about six inches long," Mr. Wakefield said.

"Good work," Elizabeth said. She got ready to cast again. "Look out, fish. Here I come!"

CHAPTER 4

Charades

Jessica heard Elizabeth, Steven, and Mr. Wakefield coming back from the dock. She put the napkins and paper plates on the table and ran to meet them.

"Did you catch anything?" she called.

"Steven did," Elizabeth said.

"It might not be the biggest fish in the lake, but it's a good start," Mr. Wakefield said.

Steven grinned as he opened his basket. He pointed to the fish inside. "Pretty cool, huh?"

"Don't come too close," Jessica said. "It's pretty. Did you catch anything, Liz?"

The others started laughing. Mrs. Wakefield heard them and came out on the porch. "What's so funny?" she asked.

Steven nudged Elizabeth. "Tell them."

Elizabeth smiled and took a deep breath. "One of the times I cast my line, I felt a tug," she began. Elizabeth pretended to reel in an imaginary line. Steven started laughing, but Elizabeth shushed him before she went on. "I was reeling it in, and I knew it was a monster fish—"

"Really?" Jessica interrupted her sister. She almost wished she had been there.

"I finally pulled it out of the water," Elizabeth said. "And—" she looked around. "It was just a monster clump of weeds."

Jessica and Mrs. Wakefield laughed. "Well,

I'm glad Steven caught something," Mrs. Wakefield said. "Why don't you three get washed up, and I'll prepare Steven's fish."

Jessica followed her sister and brother inside. She could tell that they had had a lot of fun. All she had done was help her mother unpack the groceries. *That* wasn't very much fun at all.

"Did you talk to Jilly?" Elizabeth asked her.

Jessica nodded. "Yes. A little. Then she had to help her mom. Jilly's nice."

"The whole family seems nice," Mrs. Wakefield added. "I invited them over to play charades after dinner."

"Oh! My favorite game!" Jessica said, jumping up and down. She had just learned the game and couldn't wait to play.

Steven laughed. "That's because you love to act."

27

Jessica ignored her brother. "I hope Jilly likes to play charades," she said.

The Crawfords came over after dinner. Mr. and Mrs. Crawford told funny stories, and Tom and Ricky talked about their Little League team. Jessica sat next to Jilly.

"It's time to play charades," Jessica said. "You like to play, don't you?"

Jilly nodded. "Yes, but nobody's allowed to do anything really hard."

"That's when it's fun," Jessica said. "I like trying to guess the answer, but I like acting out the clues even more."

"So do I," Jilly said.

"Who wants to do the first charade?" Mr. Crawford asked.

Jessica was about to say "me!" when Jilly called out. "I get to go first."

"But—" Jessica began. She didn't say anything more.

"OK," Jilly said. She opened her hands like a book. "That means book."

"We know that," Steven said.

Jilly frowned at him. Then she held up three fingers. "That means three words."

"We know that, too," Ricky said.

Jessica sat lower in her chair. Jilly was spoiling all the fun. While the others guessed, Jilly kept scolding them. She was very impatient with everyone. Jessica hoped it would be her turn soon.

"Tell me what you're going to pick," Jilly whispered in Jessica's ear before Jessica stood up in front of everyone.

"No!" Jessica shook her head. "You have to guess."

Jilly crossed her arms and pouted. "That's not nice."

Jessica saw that Elizabeth had overheard them. She gave her sister a smile. She was beginning to think that playing with Jilly might not be much fun after all.

CHAPTER 5

Jessica's Bad Dream

That night, Jessica had a dream. She was in a rowboat with a fishing pole in the bottom. She was rowing and rowing as hard as she could, but the boat wouldn't go forward. Then she heard a splash behind her. She turned to look, but nothing was there. Another splash came from the other side, but again, she didn't see anything.

Jessica knew it was a fish.

She tried to row again. She had to get away from the fish and all the strange splashes around her. She knew that the fish were angry at her, because they didn't want her to catch them.

Then she thought she saw something out of the corner of her eye. It looked like a shark!

"There's a giant fish in the lake!" she yelled.

She picked up the oars again and tried to row. The boat still wouldn't move. She rowed faster and faster, but the monster fish was catching up to her. She had to get away!

Suddenly, Jessica woke up and sat up in bed. The room was very dark. Her heart was pounding.

"What's wrong?" Elizabeth asked from the top bunk.

Jessica took a deep breath. She was still scared.

"Nothing," she whispered. It sounded silly

33

to say she was being chased by a fish. Besides, she didn't want her sister to know she was afraid of them. "I was having a bad dream," she said.

Jessica curled up under the covers again and closed her eyes. Even though she knew sharks lived in the ocean and not in lakes, she definitely wasn't going fishing now.

In the morning, everyone woke up bright and early. They ate breakfast outside on the picnic table. The Crawfords were eating outside, too.

"This is going to be our big fishing day," Mr. Wakefield said. "We'll take the boat out into the middle of the lake."

Jessica stirred her cereal with her spoon. She wasn't sure what to do.

"Can we go swimming, too?" Elizabeth asked.

Mrs. Wakefield nodded. "Of course. I'll make sandwiches, and we can stay out on the lake all day."

"All right!" shouted Steven.

Jessica looked at her mother. "Mom? Do I have to go?"

Mrs. Wakefield's smile faded. "Dear, you can't stay here by yourself."

"Excuse me," Mrs. Crawford called out. "I couldn't help overhearing. Jessica can stay with me and Jilly. We're not going fishing."

Jessica wasn't sure she wanted to spend the day with bossy Jilly, but anything was better than fishing. "Can I stay, Mom? Please?" she asked.

"If it's what you want, then yes," Mrs. Wakefield said.

"Thanks." Jessica let out a sigh of relief.

Mr. and Mrs. Wakefield, Steven, and Elizabeth carried their picnic basket and fishing gear down to the dock and got into the boat. Jessica, Jilly, and Mrs. Crawford waved good-bye from the dock.

"Now we can play all day," Jessica said happily. "Did you bring any dolls?"

Jilly nodded. "Yes, but I can't let you play with them. You might get them dirty."

"No, I won't. I'll take good care of them," Jessica promised. She threw a stick into the water.

"Hey, you splashed me," Jilly said as she looked down at her dress.

Jessica put one hand over her mouth. "Oops. Sorry. It was an accident."

"You'd better not do that again," Jilly said.

"I said I was sorry," Jessica grumbled.

"OK. Come on," Jilly said. "Let's play school. I'll be the teacher."

Jessica made a face when Jilly's back was turned. Then she looked out at the lake. She could see her whole family in the boat, and she could hear them laughing.

She was beginning to wonder if she had made a big mistake.

CHAPTER 6

Elizabeth's Lucky Day

Elizabeth popped a raisin into her mouth. "Do you think we'll catch a lot of fish today?" she asked.

"Yes," Mrs. Wakefield said. She was opening a plastic bag full of little pieces of meat.

"Is that lunch or bait?" Mr. Wakefield asked.

Mrs. Wakefield laughed. "What do you think?"

"Lunch, I guess. I'm starved," he said.

"You just had breakfast, silly," Mrs. Wakefield said.

Elizabeth smiled. She loved it when her parents joked around. She cast her line. She was sure today would be her lucky day. Steven was on the other side of the boat, and the Crawfords were a short distance away in their boat. It was getting hot. Elizabeth was about to ask her mother for a can of juice, but then she felt a tug.

"I got a bite!" she said. She tried to remember all the things her father had told her. She reeled in carefully.

"I hope it's not more weeds," Steven said.

Mrs. Wakefield put one finger to her lips. "Shh."

Elizabeth concentrated hard on reeling in her line. At last, she pulled a very large fish out of the water.

"Look!" she yelled. "I got a fish!"

"Congratulations! It's quite a nice-looking

trout," Mr. Wakefield said. "First catch of the day goes to Elizabeth!"

Elizabeth saw Tom and Ricky looking in her direction. They waved. It was fun to be the center of attention, but she wished Jessica was with them.

For another hour, everyone was busy fishing. Elizabeth caught another trout, but she threw it back in. "We only need enough for dinner," she reminded her family.

Soon, they had all caught at least one fish each. They kept the biggest ones, and let the others go.

"I'm getting hot," Steven announced.

"Go for a swim, then," Mr. Wakefield said.

Steven took off his jeans and T-shirt. He was wearing his bathing suit underneath. He stood up and jumped over the side of the boat.

"Steven!" Elizabeth laughed. She leaned

over to watch him come back up. "Isn't it cold?"

Steven pushed his wet hair out of his eyes. "It's freezing! Come on in, you guys!" he yelled at the Crawfords.

Ricky and Tom finished reeling in and jumped in the water, too. Mr. and Mrs. Wakefield and Mr. Crawford watched the boys.

"Don't swim too far away from the boats, kids," Mr. Wakefield warned.

Elizabeth took her T-shirt off. Her bathing suit was underneath. "Watch out!" she yelled. She jumped into the water from the front of the boat.

As soon as she shot up to the surface, she screamed. "Yiii! It's cold!"

"Let's race around the boats," Steven said.

Ricky, Tom, and Steven began a swimming

race, but Elizabeth climbed back into the boat. "Brrr," she said, shivering.

"Here's a towel," her mother said. "Do you want to eat your lunch now?"

Elizabeth nodded. She wrapped the towel around her shoulders and took a peanut-butter sandwich from her mother. While she ate it, she looked at the water and at the trees on the mountains. A flock of wild geese flew overhead. She couldn't remember ever having so much fun.

"I wish Jessica were here," she said.

"So do we," Mr. Wakefield told her, opening a can of soda. "Maybe she'll join us tomorrow."

"I don't want her to miss out on all the fun," Elizabeth added.

Mrs. Wakefield kissed her cheek. "You're

sweet to say that. But Jessica's playing with Jilly today. I'm sure they're having a lot of fun, too."

"I guess so," Elizabeth agreed slowly. Deep inside, though, she didn't know how anyone could have fun playing with Jilly Crawford.

CHAPTER 7

Jessica's Unlucky Day

Jessica picked up Jilly's teddy bear, but Jilly took it away from her quickly.

"You can't use the bear," Jilly said.

"Why not?" Jessica was getting angrier by the minute. "I can't touch your dolls. I can't touch your china set. And now you won't let me touch your bear. Why?"

"Because I'm using it," Jilly explained.

Jessica sat down on the porch. She put her elbows on her knees and her chin in her hands. She was having a terrible time. She wished she had brought some of her own dolls.

Jessica sighed and looked out at the lake. A boat was coming back to the dock. It was her family.

"I have to go!" she yelled as she started running down to the lake.

Her feet went "thunk-thunk-thunk" on the wooden dock. "Hi!" she called, waving both arms over her head.

"Ahoy, Jessica!" Mr. Wakefield shouted.

Jessica hopped up and down with impatience while they rowed in. Finally the boat bumped up against the wooden ladder.

"You were gone so long," Jessica said.

"We had a lot of fun, Jess," Elizabeth told her, as she climbed out. "We went swimming over the side of the boat, and we threw our bread crusts to the geese. We even saw some swans."

"And we caught lots of fish," Steven added. "But we only kept five. Enough for dinner."

Mr. Wakefield put the picnic basket up on the dock. "We missed you, Jessica."

"We sure did," Mrs. Wakefield agreed. "Did you have a good time with Jilly?"

Jessica bit her lip. Part of her wanted them to feel bad for having had fun without her. But part of her didn't want them to know that she had had a terrible time playing with Jilly.

"It was OK," she said.

"Do you think you'll want to come with us tomorrow?" Elizabeth asked hopefully. "It's really, really a lot of fun. Besides, it'll be our last day, and you have to go fishing at least once. Please? Pretty please?"

"Come on, Jessica," Mrs. Wakefield said. "Give it a try."

Mr. Wakefield smoothed her hair. "It won't hurt."

"OK," Jessica agreed. "I'll come tomorrow."

Elizabeth stared at her in surprise. "You will? Really?"

"You're not going to get another stomach-ache?" Steven teased her. "Or get seasick?"

"No," Jessica said.

She helped her family unpack the boat. Now she couldn't remember why she had made such a fuss about going fishing. After all, they threw most of the fish back into the water. Anyway, it had to be better than stay-ing behind and playing with Jilly for another day.

"Tomorrow we'll get up at the crack of dawn and get out on the lake early," Mrs.

Wakefield said. "That way we'll have a good day of fishing, and then we can drive home without rushing."

That night, they cooked the fresh trout over a campfire. The fish had a lot of small bones in them, which they had to take out carefully as they ate. Dinner was delicious.

"You're really going to come fishing tomorrow, right?" Elizabeth asked as they got ready for bed.

"Yes," Jessica said. She crossed her heart and snapped her fingers twice. It was their special promise sign.

"Who knows?" she added. "Maybe I'll even catch a fish."

CHAPTER 8

Family Fun

When Elizabeth woke up, it was still dark out. She could hear her parents getting breakfast ready. She leaned over the side of the bunk.

"Jessie!" she whispered. "Time to get up."

Jessica mumbled and rolled over.

Jessica always woke up slowly. Elizabeth climbed down the ladder and sat on the side of Jessica's bed. "Time to get up," she said again.

"I'm sleepy," Jessica said from under the covers.

Elizabeth finished getting dressed, while Jessica stayed in bed. "Come on," Elizabeth said, tapping Jessica's shoulder.

Jessica kicked her blanket back. "I don't feel well," she said. "I have a sore throat.

"Oh, no!" Elizabeth was so surprised and disappointed that she didn't know what else to say. Was Jessica pretending to be sick again to get out of going fishing?

"But you promised!" Elizabeth said sadly. "Do you really, really have a sore throat?"

Jessica sat up in bed. "I really, really do," she said. Her voice sounded hoarse. She made their secret promise sign. "My throat hurts. It's hard to swallow."

"I'll tell Mom and Dad," Elizabeth said. If Jessica promised, then she really did have a sore throat. It wasn't just another excuse.

"Good morning," Mrs. Wakefield said

when Elizabeth walked into the cabin kitchen.

Elizabeth saw that her mother had already made sandwiches to take in the boat. "Jessica has a sore throat," said said quickly.

"What?" Mr. Wakefield put down the coffee pot and stared at her.

"She really does," Elizabeth said.

"Well, it might be from the dampness," her mother said. "Tell Jessica to go ahead and get dressed."

Mr. Wakefield held up one hand. "Wait a second. I'll go see how she is." He walked with Elizabeth back into the bedroom. "Jessica? Do you feel like you want to stay here today?"

"No," Jessica said. She pushed the covers back and leaned on her elbow. She tried swallowing a couple of times. "I *want* to go fishing."

Elizabeth looked at her sister. Just thinking about Jessica's sore throat made her own throat hurt. She swallowed hard.

Jessica still seemed sleepy during breakfast, but she said she wanted to go fishing. They all got in the boat and shoved off. The sun was starting to come up.

"It's going to be a lot of fun," Elizabeth promised her sister. "Now you'll get to see the swans."

"I can't wait," Jessica said, smiling.

Everything was very quiet on the water. Mist hung in the air and swirled around the boat.

"Let's go to that inlet where the tree roots stick out of the water," Steven said. "I'll bet the fish are biting there."

"Good idea," Mr. Wakefield said.

Elizabeth and Steven took turns rowing.

Jessica took a turn, too, but she was so slow that Steven got impatient. Soon, they reached the quiet hideaway on the opposite side of the lake.

"This is your pole, Jess," Elizabeth said, handing Jessica the lightest one. "All you have to do is put a little piece of meat on the hook. Like this."

Jessica watched while Elizabeth baited her hook. "Now what?" she asked.

"First you bring it back over your shoulder, and then you swing it," Elizabeth explained. "Make sure you let go of the wheel, or nothing will happen."

Jessica took a few practice swings without letting go of the wheel. "OK, this time I'll let it go."

Elizabeth held her breath and watched. Jessica put the pole over her shoulder and moved her thumb away from the crank on the handle. Then she swung the tip of the pole out in front of her. The hook and line went "zzzz" out over the water and plopped in with a little splash.

"Good cast, Jessica," Mrs. Wakefield said. "Now reel it in slowly, and see if anything happens."

Jessica turned the crank slowly, until the hook came back up out of the water.

"This time, try to cast it out near those logs," Elizabeth said. "The fish like to hide under there."

"OK," Jessica said. She looked at Elizabeth and smiled. "This is fun."

Elizabeth crossed her fingers. The most fun of all would be if Jessica caught a fish.

CHAPTER 9

The Biggest Fish
in the Lake

Jessica hunched her shoulders. She felt a little bit chilly, and each time she swallowed, her throat hurt.

"How's that throat of yours?" her father asked in a soft voice. They all talked quietly on the boat, so as not to scare the fish away.

"It still hurts," Jessica said. "But I don't mind."

Jessica sniffed, but didn't say anything more. She didn't want them to think she was complaining. She didn't want anyone to call her a crybaby, either. She was determined to prove that she liked to fish now.

"Try another cast, Jessica," Mrs. Wakefield said.

"OK." She looked at everyone. "Watch this. Even if I don't catch anything, I'm getting better at casting."

"You do it better than I do now," Elizabeth said.

Jessica took a deep breath. She brought her pole back and then cast it forward. Her hook went whizzing through the air and landed right next to a sunken log.

"Good shot!" Steven said. "There's probably a big old fish sitting right there."

"I hope so," Jessica said. She grinned and gave a little tug on her line, then turned the crank a tiny bit. She was trying to imagine what it was like to be a fish down in the water, when something pulled on her line.

"Hey!" she gasped. "I think I have something!"

Everyone watched Jessica. "Just bring it in nice and steady," Mr. Wakefield said.

"Do you want me to do it for you?" Elizabeth offered.

Jessica shook her head. "No way!" she said, holding her pole tightly. "Even if it's just seaweed, I want to pull it out all by myself."

"Whatever it is, don't let it get away," Steven said.

"I won't," Jessica said. She could feel something pulling hard on the other end of her fishing line. It was trying to get away, but Jessica was not going to let it.

61

"I'll get you," she whispered.

Her arms were getting tired. She had a feeling it must be a very big fish, because it was pulling very hard on her pole. She cranked some more. Mrs. Wakefield reached out with the net.

"That's it, Jessica," Mr. Wakefield whispered. "You're almost there."

Jessica yanked her pole up in the air. A very large speckled trout was twisting and spinning on the end of her line! Her mother quickly caught it in the net.

"Look at what I got!" Jessica shouted. Shouting made her throat hurt, but she didn't care.

"That's the biggest catch of the weekend," Steven said. "I can't believe you caught it, Jessica!"

"I can," Elizabeth said proudly. "That must be the biggest fish in the lake."

Jessica was so pleased that she couldn't stop smiling. Now nobody would say she was a crybaby or a spoilsport. She was a champion fisher!

"Ned, get the camera out," Mrs. Wakefield said to Mr. Wakefield. "We have to have a picture of Jessica and her fish."

"I think I'll call him Jumbo," Jessica announced. She took the net from her mother. Jumbo was very heavy. Jessica looked at him through the net. His skin was smooth and shiny. Each scale was like a piece of brown glass.

"Hold him up while I snap the picture, Jessica," Mrs. Wakefield said. "Say cheese."

Steven helped Jessica hold up Jumbo.

"FISH!" Jessica said as the camera went off.

Everyone laughed, and Jessica took another look at her prize trout. She could see his gills open and shut while he tried to breathe in the air. "I want him to keep on being the biggest fish in the lake," Jessica said. "I'm putting him back in."

Mr. Wakefield carefully took the hook out of Jumbo's mouth.

While the rest of the family watched, Jessica tipped the net upside down over the water. Jumbo fell in with a splash. Jessica leaned over to watch him swim away.

"'Bye, Jumbo," she called. "I'm glad I caught him," she said happily. "And I'm glad I let him go, too."

She would never be afraid to fish again.

CHAPTER 10

Sore Throats

"Yahoo!" Elizabeth cheered. Then she quickly put her hand to her throat. Yelling made it hurt.

"What's wrong?" Mrs. Wakefield asked.

Elizabeth tried swallowing. "I think I have a sore throat, too," she said.

"You do?" Jessica asked.

Their parents looked at each other.

"I think we should take a closer look at the two of you," Mrs. Wakefield said, sounding worried.

Elizabeth and Jessica opened their mouths

wide so their mother could look in. Elizabeth was beginning to get a headache. She felt cold, too.

"Uh-oh," Mrs. Wakefield said. She looked down Jessica's throat. "Oh, honey. That throat looks red. I'm afraid I didn't quite believe you before."

Jessica sniffed. "That's OK, Mom. I guess you thought it was like my stomachache," she said.

"Well, I really apologize, sweetheart," Mrs. Wakefield said, giving Jessica a hug. "You both have very red throats and swollen tonsils."

"Tonsils?" Elizabeth's stomach did a swan dive. She knew that when kids got tonsillitis, they usually had to go to the hospital and have their tonsils taken out.

"Do we have to have an operation?" Jessica asked nervously.

67

Mr. Wakefield started rowing back toward the dock. "Let's not jump to any conclusions. We'll drive home right away, and then we can make an appointment to see Dr. Wolf first thing tomorrow."

"Hey, that means they get to miss school," Steven said. "I think my tonsils hurt, too."

Mrs. Wakefield gave him a stern look. Steven shrugged. "Just kidding."

Elizabeth had felt sorry for Jessica, because she knew how much her sister's throat hurt. But her own throat was hurting more and more all the time. Each swallow was more difficult.

"Are you scared?" Jessica whispered to her sister. "What if we have to go to the hospital?"

"Maybe we won't," Elizabeth whispered

68

back. "But it's too bad we have to leave early."

"I know," Jessica said. "I'm just glad I finally went fishing. Bossy old Jilly wouldn't even give it a try. Can you believe that?"

Elizabeth smiled at her sister. She loved her twin sister more than anyone else in the world. And she was glad they were getting tonsillitis at the same time. If she had to have an operation, she sure didn't want to have it alone!

Will Jessica and Elizabeth have to go to the hospital? Find out in Sweet Valley Kids #20, THE TWINS GO TO THE HOSPITAL.

LOOKIN' COOL IN YOUR SWEET VALLEY™ SUNGLASSES

Reading books is one of the coolest things you can do. But you'll be even cooler in your awesome new SWEET VALLEY™ SUNGLASSES. All SWEET VALLEY™ SUNGLASSES give UV protection, and the frames are made of durable, impact resistant plastic. The glasses have incredible COLOR MAGIC frames that actually change color in sunlight, and each pair of glasses will be imprinted with the SWEET VALLEY™ insignia. SWEET VALLEY™ SUNGLASSES are totally cool and totally free to the first 10,000 kids we hear from who've purchased a SWEET VALLEY™ book containing this coupon. If you want a pair, fill in the coupon below (no photocopies or facsimilies allowed), cut it out and send it to:

SWEET VALLEY™ SUNGLASSES
BANTAM BOOKS, YOUNG READERS MARKETING, Dept. IG,
666 Fifth Avenue, New York, New York 10103

- -

If mine is one of the first 10,000 coupons you receive, please send my
SWEET VALLEY™ SUNGLASSES to:

Name_____Birth Date:_____

Address_____

City/State/Prov._____

Zip/Postal Code_____

Offer open only to residents of the United States, Puerto Rico and Canada. Void where prohibited, taxed and restricted. Please allow six to eight weeks for shipment. Offer expires June 30, 1991. Bantam is not responsible for lost, incompletely identified or misdirected requests. If your coupon is not among the first 10,000 received, we will not be able to send you the Sunglasses.

SVK-1 6/91

SWEET VALLEY TWINS

Buy them at your local bookstore or use this handy page for ordering:

Bantam Books, Dept. SVT3, 414 East Golf Road, Des Plaines, IL 60016

Please send me the items I have checked above. I am enclosing $_____
(please add $2.50 to cover postage and handling). Send check or money
order, no cash or C.O.D.s please.

Mr/Ms _____

Address _____

City/State_____ Zip_____

SVT3-2/91

Please allow four to six weeks for delivery.
Prices and availability subject to change without notice.